D0574800

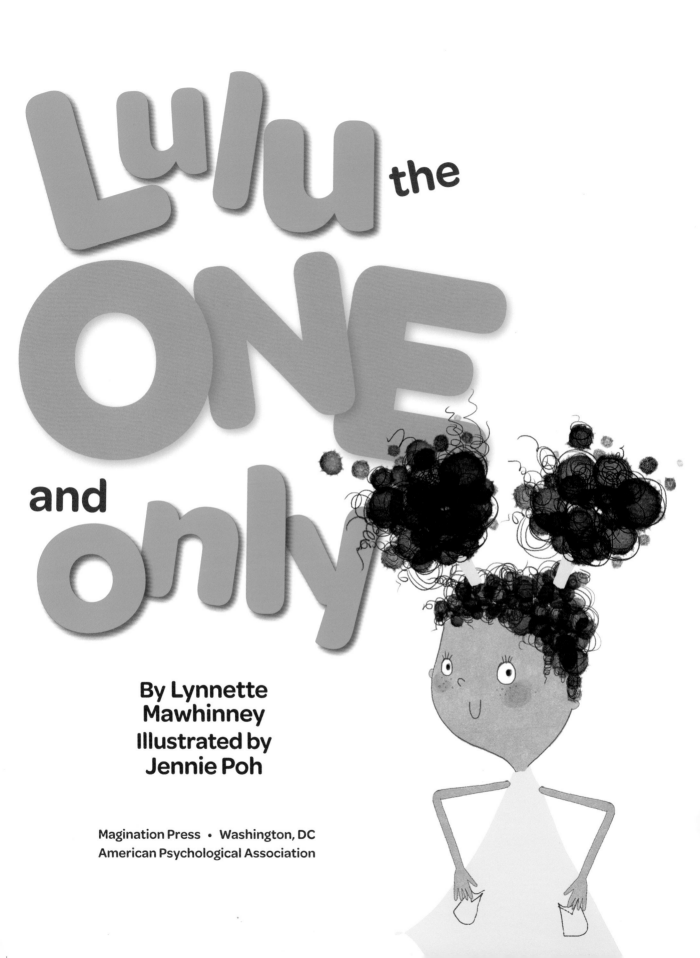

Lulu the ONE and only

By Lynnette Mawhinney

Illustrated by Jennie Poh

Magination Press • Washington, DC
American Psychological Association

In loving memory of my daughter, Amelia Jane Wangui Gachoki—*LM*

For Aurelia and Evangeline—*JP*

Books for Kids From the
American Psychological Association

Copyright © 2020 by Magination Press, an imprint of the
American Psychological Association. All rights reserved.
Illustrations copyright © 2020 by Jennie Poh. Except as
permitted under the United States Copyright Act of 1976,
no part of this publication may be reproduced or distributed
in any form or by any means, or stored in a database or
retrieval system, without the prior written permission of
the publisher.

Magination Press is a registered trademark of the American
Psychological Association. Order books at maginationpress.org,
or call 1-800-374-2721.

Book design by Gwen Grafft
Printed by Sonic Media Solutions, Inc., Medford, NY

Library of Congress Cataloging-in-Publication Data
Names: Mawhinney, Lynnette, 1979- author. | Poh, Jennie,
    illustrator.
Title: Lulu the one and only / by Lynnette Mawhinney, PhD ;
    illustrated by Jennie Poh.
Description: Washington, DC : Magination Press, [2020] |
    "American Psychological Association." | Summary: Lulu gets
    help from her brother, Zane, to respond to other people's
    confusion about her racial identity by using a "power
    phrase" to declare who she is, rather than what.
Identifiers: LCCN 2019043244 | ISBN 9781433831591
    (hardcover)
Subjects: CYAC: Racially mixed people—Fiction. |
    Prejudices—Fiction. | Individuality—Fiction. | Family
    life—Fiction.
Classification: LCC PZ7.1.M384 Lul 2020 | DDC [E]—dc23
LC record available at https://lccn.loc.gov/2019043244

Manufactured in the United States of America
10 9 8 7 6 5 4 3 2 1

My name is Luliwa Lovington, but everyone
calls me Lulu. It means "pearl" in Arabic.

Mama tells me, "You are unique and gorgeous, just like a black pearl." She wears these beautiful earrings all the time. They are from her mother in Kenya.

My big brother's name is Zane, and it means "gift."
He is silly, and he makes me laugh a lot.

Being in a part Black and part White family seems to confuse people around us. They say a lot of mean things to us because they think we don't fit in.

Kids tease Zane. "You're the blackest guy on the team."
"The coach is *really* your dad?"

When I play in the park, the other
moms always think Mama is my sitter.
"What do you charge?
We are looking for one."

When I'm out with Daddy, some people think I'm adopted. "That's so nice that you gave her a good home. Where did she come from?"

Everyone else might be confused,
but I'm not. I love our family.

But being a mix of Mama and Daddy always brings around THAT question.

I hate THAT question.

"What are you?"

"What are you?"

"Zane, do people ever ask you what you are?"

"Yeah. It's annoying. But that's when I use my power phrase."

"Your power phrase?"

"It helps people understand *who* you are, not *what* you are.

I'm proud of our family and that I'm brown, but I am more than my skin.

I want people to know what's inside me too. When I get THAT question, I tell people:

I'm magic

made from

my parents.

Dad taught me how to play hockey, and I love to study space because of Mom. You know how good I am at so many things. Mom and Dad have a ton to do with that."

Wow. Zane is really smart.
Now I need a power phrase, too.
And I need it fast.

But how do I find *my* power phrase?

The question is not what
I am, but who I am.

I am a good singer.
I am fast and strong.
I am loving and kind.
I am a black pearl,
unique and gorgeous.

I've got to get this right!

The next day, Billy asked,
"Hey Lulu—what are you?"

It was time.

I'm **Lulu Lovington**, the **ONE** and **only!**

"Cool," said Billy. "Do you like to sing?"

We sat together
at lunch and sang
our favorite songs.

The real treasure is inside.
Just like an oyster holds a pearl.

And just like me.

Lulu Lovington, the ONE and Only!

Author's Note

Lulu's and Zane's experiences as mixed race children are quite common. There are currently an estimated seven million people in the United States who identify as biracial, multiracial, or mixed race. Millions of Americans deal with THAT question, *What are you?*, on a daily basis—just like Lulu. The power phrase is a tool designed to help mixed race children learn how to navigate their emotions and responses to this question.

Lulu was fortunate to have Zane help her to understand what to do in these instances. But that might not be the case for some children, as they may not have a fellow biracial sibling. I know that was true of my own experiences, as I was the only biracial person in my family. There are many beauties to being mixed race, but one complexity is that both parents do not share the same identity as their children. It is often hard for parents to understand the perspective of their children, and sometimes mixed-race children can feel alone in their experiences. There are certain practices that can assist in the emotional development of biracial children.

- **Talk about race.** Even in multiracial families, parents may avoid dialogues about race. Do not be afraid to talk about race and all the complexities that come as a family. This helps children to establish a language around race while having the opportunity to articulate their emotions in a safe environment.

- **Listen.** Since biracial children have experiences that may be different than your own, do not feel obligated to act as though you understand their perspective. Sometimes children just need to be heard, valued, and feel supported in their experiences.

- **Work on developing self-love.** Unfortunately, there is no escaping THAT question. Self-love is critical in instances when your child is challenged for how he or she looks. Self-love is an intentional process. The power phrase helps children embrace self-love when others might challenge who they are.